CARTER HIGH
SENIOR YEAR

WORST
Year Ever

By Eleanor Robins

SADDLEBACK
EDUCATIONAL PUBLISHING

CARTER HIGH
SENIOR YEAR

EDUCATIONAL PUBLISHING
www.sdlback.com

Copyright ©2005, 2011 by Saddleback Educational Publishing

ISBN-13: 978-1-61651-330-6
ISBN-10: 1-61651-330-6
eBook: 978-1-60291-978-5

Printed in Guangzhou, China
0910/09-42-10

15 14 13 12 11   1 2 3 4 5

Chapter 1

It was the first day of school. Griff had just arrived at school. He was very early. It was the first time he was ever early to school.

Griff could hardly wait for school to start. It was his senior year. And he waited a long time to be a senior.

He started to go in the school.

Steve came out the door. He had been in some of Griff's classes last year. And Steve had run with Griff during the summer.

"Hi, Griff. Why are you here so early?" Steve asked.

"I waited a long time to be a senior. And I can hardly wait for this year to start," Griff said.

Steve said, "I feel the same way."

"Where are you going?" Griff asked.

"I'm going to the track. I found out who my first teacher is. So now I am going to run some laps," Steve said.

Steve was on the track team.

Griff had tried out for track last year. But he didn't have the grades to be on the team. It was all because Mr. Reese had failed him. Mr. Reese was his science teacher.

Steve asked, "Who do you have for your first class? Do you know yet?"

Griff said, "No. I am going to try to find out now."

"I have Mrs. Dodd," Steve said.

Griff didn't know who she was.

"Is she new?" Griff asked.

"Yes," Steve said.

Griff hoped he didn't get her. He didn't like new teachers. He wanted to know how much work they made students do. But there was no way to find that out.

Steve asked, "Do you want to run some laps with me? You can go find out who your teacher is. I will wait for you. Then we can run some laps."

Griff knew he had time to run laps with Steve. Maybe he should do it. He was worried about the first day of school. And maybe it would help him to run some laps. Then he wouldn't worry as much about school.

But Ben called out to Steve. Ben was Steve's best friend.

Ben said, "Steve, come with me. I am on my way to the track."

Griff didn't like Ben. Last year Griff had liked Laine. He had wanted to ask her for a date. But he couldn't make himself do it.

Then Ben had asked Laine for a date. They started to date. It was too late for Griff to ask her.

Griff thought they still dated. But he didn't know that for sure.

Steve asked, "How about it, Griff? Do you want to run with us? We can wait for you."

"No," Griff said.

Griff didn't want to run with Ben. Last year, he sometimes ate lunch with Ben. But he didn't want to do that now. Not after Ben dated Laine.

Steve said, "OK. Maybe you'll join us next time. I need to get to the track. I will see you later."

Steve ran over to Ben. The two boys

ran off to the track.

Just his luck. School hadn't even started. And Griff had already seen Ben.

His year wasn't getting off to a good start.

Chapter 2

Griff went in the school. He saw Mr. Reese.

Mr. Reese was walking down the hall. He had some class cards.

Griff looked the other way. He didn't want to speak to Mr. Reese.

Mr. Reese said, "Hi, Griff."

Mr. Reese stopped. He acted as if he wanted to talk to Griff. So Griff had to stop too.

Why did Mr. Reese want to talk to him?

"Hi," Griff said.

But Griff didn't sound glad to see Mr. Reese.

Mr. Reese had failed him last year. That meant Griff couldn't be on the track team. Griff had to go to school all summer. He took the science class again.

Griff was glad Mr. Reese didn't teach summer school. And he was glad Mr. Reese didn't teach seniors. He would never have Mr. Reese for a teacher again.

"I am glad to see you, Griff," Mr. Reese said.

"Why?" Griff asked.

"I wanted to talk to you before school started," Mr. Reese said.

"Why?" Griff asked.

But he wasn't sure he wanted to know why.

"You are in my first class this semester," Mr. Reese said.

"I am?" Griff asked.

"Yes," Mr. Reese said.

Mr. Reese had to be wrong. Griff couldn't be in his class.

"But I went to summer school. I took that science class again. And I passed it," Griff said.

"I know you did, Griff," Mr. Reese said.

"Then I can't be in your class. I am a senior now," Griff said.

"I am teaching seniors this year," Mr. Reese said.

"You can't," Griff said before he could stop himself.

Mr. Reese said, "But I am, Griff. And Coach Mann is going to teach seniors too. He will be a P.E. teacher this year."

Coach Mann was the track coach. He found out Griff didn't have the grades. So he took Griff off the track team last year. Griff had him for English too. He gave Griff a hard time.

Griff hoped he wouldn't get Coach Mann this year. His luck couldn't be that bad.

Mr. Reese said, "I want you to study a lot, Griff. You are smart. You should have passed my class last year. But you didn't study."

Griff did study. He studied a little. But Mr. Reese made his students study too much.

Why did he have to have Mr. Reese again?

So he would have Mr. Reese for science again. But it was worse. He would have him for his first class. Griff's day would get off to a bad start.

Griff could go to the office. He could try to get a new teacher. But it wouldn't do any good. He tried that last year. He didn't get out of Mr. Reese's class. So he was sure he wouldn't be able to this year.

"Would you like to have your class card now, Griff? Or shall you pick it up in class?" Mr. Reese asked.

"Now," Griff said.

Mr. Reese gave Griff his class card.

Then Mr. Reese said, "See you in class, Griff."

Then Mr. Reese walked on down the hall.

Why did Mr. Reese have to teach seniors?

It wasn't fair.

They shouldn't let teachers change grades. It wasn't fair to the students.

He would never pass his senior year. Not with Mr. Reese as his science teacher. And he wouldn't get to graduate with his class. Griff would have to go back to summer school.

Or it could be worse. He might have to go to school next fall.

What a way to start the first day of his senior year.

Chapter 3

Joe walked up to Griff. He asked, "What's wrong, Griff? What did Mr. Reese say to you?"

Mr. Reese had failed Joe last year too. Joe had been in summer school with Griff.

"Mr. Reese is going to teach seniors this year. And I am in his class," Griff said.

Joe said, "Oh, no. I sure hope I don't get him. Who else do you have?"

Griff looked at his class card. He had Coach Mann too. How could his luck be that bad?

Joe asked, "What's wrong? Who else did you get?"

"I got Coach Mann for P.E.," Griff said.

"What is bad about that? I had him for English last year. He was OK," Joe said.

"I had him too. But he doesn't like me," Griff said.

Joe looked very surprised. He asked, "Why do you think that?"

"I don't want to talk about it," Griff said.

Joe said, "OK. Too bad that you have Coach Mann and Mr. Reese. I am going to find out who I have. I will see you later."

"OK," Griff said.

Joe hurried down the hall.

Griff went to Mr. Reese's classroom. He wanted to be there before the other students came. And he wanted to sit in the back row. Griff knew he was going to fail the class. So why should he sit near the front?

Mr. Reese smiled at Griff. He said, "I am glad you came early, Griff. Take a front seat. You can listen better there."

Griff wasn't going to sit in the front row. But he couldn't sit in the back row now. So he sat in the second row.

Ed came into class. Ed had been in some of Griff's classes last year. Ed always made all As. And he always knew everything. Griff was sure Ed didn't care who his teacher was.

Maybe Ed would sit in front of him. Griff hoped he would. Griff might need some help. And maybe Ed would help him.

"Hi, Ed," Griff said.

"Hi," Ed said.

Ed sat down in the front row. But he didn't sit in front of Griff.

Joe came in. He sat down behind Griff. Joe asked, "Can you believe our bad luck? I got Mr. Reese again for science too."

"Too bad," Griff said.

It seemed as if his luck was bad more times than good.

And it got worse because Ben came in. Why did Ben have to be in his class? Ben sat on the other side of the room. And Griff was glad he did.

More students came in.

Mr. Reese said, "It is almost time for class to start. Finish up your talking. Let's get ready to work."

Laine came in. Laine had been in his history class last year. Griff hoped she wouldn't be in one of his classes this year.

Only two desks were left. One was in front of Griff. The other was in front of Ben.

Mr. Reese said, "Find a seat quickly, Laine. It is time for class to start."

Griff didn't want Laine to sit in front

of him. And he was sure she wouldn't. She would sit in front of Ben.

Laine quickly looked around. Then she surprised Griff. She sat down in front of him.

Griff knew Laine saw him. But she didn't speak to him.

And there was no way Griff would speak to her first.

Laine didn't like him. Griff was sure about that. So why did she sit in front of him? Didn't she see the desk in front of Ben?

Griff had Mr. Reese for science. He had Coach Mann for P.E. And now Laine was sitting in front of him.

His day couldn't get any worse.

Chapter 4

But Griff's day did get worse.

Mr. Reese said, "You each have a science book on your desk. I will call the roll. Answer by telling me the number of your book."

Mr. Reese called the roll. The students told him their book numbers.

Then Mr. Reese said, "Open your books to chapter 1. We will read some of it now. You need to read the rest at home. You will have a test on it next week."

It was only the first day. Mr. Reese was already talking about a test. He did that last year too.

Griff was glad when the class was over. He wanted to get out of the class as fast as he could.

He had P.E. next. But he wasn't in a hurry to get to the gym. He was just in a hurry to get out of science.

Joe said, "I have P.E. with Coach Mann next. When do you have him?"

"Next," Griff said.

"Great. We can walk to class together," Joe said.

The boys walked to the gym. They talked about what they had done since summer school. Summer school was long. So they had not had time to do much else.

They got to the gym.

Coach Mann was at the door. He was checking the roll as the students went in.

Griff hoped Coach Mann forgot that he tried out for track. And Griff hoped he forgot about the grades.

But Coach Mann said, "Hi, Griff. Are you trying out for track again this year?"

So Coach Mann hadn't forgotten. And he didn't like Griff. Griff was sure about that now.

Griff sort of laughed. But it wasn't a real laugh.

Why did he have to have Coach Mann for P.E.? He might fail that class too.

Coach Mann didn't say any more to him. Griff was glad.

Joe said, "I didn't know you were on the track team. You failed science. How did you get on the team?"

Griff didn't want to answer Joe. But he knew he might as well. Joe would keep asking until he did.

"I wasn't on the team," Griff said.

"But Coach Mann just said you tried out for the team. Was Coach Mann

wrong?" Joe asked.

"No," Griff said.

"But you didn't have the grades. So why did you try out for the team?" Joe asked.

"I didn't think Coach Mann would check my grades. But he did check them. Then he took me off the team," Griff said.

"He must have been mad at you. You should have known he would check your grades. All of the coaches have to check grades. Didn't you know that?" Joe asked.

Griff knew that. Joe didn't have to tell him.

Class started then. Griff was glad. He didn't want to talk to Joe anymore.

The rest of P.E. was OK. But Griff was glad when P.E. was over.

Joe said, "I have math next. What do you have?"

"History with Mrs. Dodd," Griff said.

"Is she new?" Joe asked.

"Yeah," Griff said.

"When do you have lunch?" Joe asked.

Griff told him.

Joe said, "Maybe I will see you at lunch."

"Yeah. Maybe," Griff said.

Griff had to go a long way to get to class. He was almost late. So he sat down at the first desk he saw.

He saw books on the desk in front of him. But no one was sitting there.

Then he saw Laine. She was on the other side of the room. She was talking to a girl. No one was sitting at the desk behind the girl. So Griff thought Laine was going to sit there.

But she didn't sit there. She stopped talking to the girl. Then she walked over to where Griff was.

Oh, no. The books must belong to her.

Laine looked at Griff before she sat down. The books were hers.

She said, "I see you are sitting behind me again."

"I didn't know you were sitting there," Griff said.

"Sure you didn't," Laine said. Then she laughed.

His day had gotten worse and worse. What a way to start his senior year.

Not only was Laine in one of his classes. But she was in two of them. Griff knew what she was thinking. She thought he liked her. And that was why he sat behind her.

He might fail P.E. He was sure he would fail science. And he wouldn't get to graduate with his class.

This would be his worst year ever.

He might as well give up now. Maybe he should drop out of school.

Chapter 5

Griff was glad when history was over.

It was lunch time. Griff was ready for lunch. Lunch might be the only class he liked this year. And it wasn't even a real class.

Griff hurried to the lunchroom. He got his lunch. Then he saw Joe. Joe was sitting at a table. Joe waved to him. Griff went to Joe's table and sat down.

Joe said, "My math class was OK. How was your history class?"

"Not so good," Griff said.

"Why?" Joe asked.

Griff said, "Mrs. Dodd gave us a lot of

homework. And we have to write a paper this semester. It isn't fair. We shouldn't have to write a paper for history."

"I sure am glad I don't have Mrs. Dodd," Joe said.

Griff wished he didn't have her too.

Joe said, "You have one teacher who doesn't like you. And you have two very hard teachers. I sure am glad I'm not you."

Why did Joe have to say that? It sure didn't make Griff feel any better.

"I am thinking about dropping out of school," Griff said.

Joe seemed very surprised.

Griff said, "I might as well. I will never pass science. And I might fail P.E. and history too. This will be my worst year ever."

Joe said, "When I got Mr. Reese again, I thought about that too. But I didn't think about it for long. My dad would never let me quit. And I am not sure I really want to quit."

Griff didn't want to quit either. But he might as well. He was going to fail. He wouldn't graduate with his class.

Joe said, "You can't quit, Griff. I need you here. I need someone to talk to about Mr. Reese. You and I are the only ones in our class that he failed."

Griff didn't say anything.

"Maybe things will get better for you. So don't quit now. Think about it for a while. OK?" Joe asked.

"Yeah. OK. I will think about it," Griff said.

Griff didn't think things would get better for him. But he could wait a few weeks. Then he would see how his grades were.

The boys ate for a few minutes. They didn't talk.

Then Joe said, "That is one cute girl over there."

"Who?" Griff asked.

Griff turned around to look at the girl. It was Laine.

Laine was looking their way. And she saw Griff looking at her. Now she would say he was looking at her in the lunchroom.

Griff quickly turned around.

"Don't you think Laine is cute?" Joe asked.

"She's OK," Griff said.

"Who does she date? Do you know?" Joe asked.

"Who cares?" Griff asked.

"I do. Maybe I will ask her for a date. What do you think?" Joe asked.

"Yeah. Fine," Griff said.

What did he care? Laine could date Ben. Or she could date Joe.

But Griff knew that wasn't true. He did care.

He liked Laine last year. And he still liked her. But he wasn't going to ask her for a date.

Griff didn't want to talk about Laine. He could hardly wait for lunch to be over.

Lunch was the only class he liked. And now he couldn't even enjoy it.

Chapter 6

It was the next week. Griff was in science class. The class was almost over.

Mr. Reese said, "You will have your first test tomorrow. It will be hard, so study for it. You are seniors this year. You don't want to fail a class."

He looked at Griff and Joe.

Griff didn't want to fail. But he knew he needed help. He didn't think he would do well on his own.

He wanted to study with Ed. But Griff didn't think Ed would study with him. And Griff wouldn't ask Laine to study with him.

Maybe Joe would study with him.

The bell rang. Griff looked back at Joe.

He asked, "Do you want to study with me, Joe?"

Joe smiled. He said, "No way. I am going to study with my girlfriend."

Joe had a new girlfriend. But she wasn't Laine. Griff was glad about that.

Griff would have to ask Ed for help. But he thought Ed would say no. It wouldn't be the first time someone didn't help him.

Ed had left the class. Griff hurried out into the hall to look for him. He saw Ed. Griff hurried over to him.

Griff asked, "OK for me to walk to class with you, Ed?"

Ed looked surprised.

"Sure. But we need to hurry," Ed said.

"OK," Griff said.

Griff always wanted to get to class on time too.

Griff could tell Ed wondered why Griff wanted to walk with him. Griff hadn't talked much to Ed last year.

The boys walked to their classes.

Griff didn't know how to ask Ed. So at first they just walked.

Then Ed asked, "Do you want to talk to me about something, Griff?"

"Yeah," Griff said.

Ed asked, "What? You need to tell me fast. I am almost to my class."

Griff still wasn't ready to ask Ed. But he knew he had to ask him.

"OK for me to study science with you sometime?" Griff asked.

Ed seemed very surprised.

He said, "I like you OK, Griff. But I don't want to study with you. You waste too much time. And you don't really care about your grades. I care about mine."

"But this is my senior year. I want to

finish school this year for sure. And I am trying to do better, Ed. I want to pass all of my classes," Griff said.

Ed didn't say anything.

But he had to let Griff study with him.

Griff asked, "What do you say, Ed? Can I study with you? I can be at your house any time you say."

Ed didn't seem happy about it. But he said, "OK, Griff. I will study with you one time. But we study at your house. Then I can leave when you start to waste time."

Griff couldn't believe it. Ed said he could study with him. Ed was an OK guy after all.

"What about today? How about after school?" Griff asked.

Ed still didn't seem happy. But he said, "OK. But I will leave when you start to waste time."

"I won't waste time. I really want to

study," Griff said.

"Where do you live?" Ed asked.

Griff told him.

"I will see you after school," said Ed.

"Thanks, Ed," Griff said.

Griff didn't think he had ever told anyone thanks before.

Chapter 7

A week went by. Griff was in science class.

Mr. Reese said, "I have graded your tests. Some of you did well. And some of you need to study more."

Griff had studied a long time with Ed. He didn't waste time. Ed even said Griff could study with him again.

Griff had thought he did OK on the test. But now he wasn't sure he did. And Griff wasn't sure he wanted to get his test back.

Mr. Reese started to pass out the tests. He gave Griff his test.

Mr. Reese said, "Good job, Griff. Keep up the good work."

Griff couldn't believe what Mr. Reese just said. He hoped Laine heard him.

Griff quickly looked at his test. He made a high C. That was a good grade for him.

After school Griff went to the track. Some days he ran on the track. School didn't seem so bad when he ran laps.

He ran two laps. Then Griff saw Coach Mann. Coach Mann was looking at him.

Coach Mann yelled to Griff. He said, "Griff. Come over here. I want to talk to you."

Griff acted as if he didn't hear Coach Mann. He didn't want to talk to Coach Mann. So he went home.

It was the next day. Griff was at P.E.

Coach Mann said, "Griff, come over here a minute. I want to talk to you."

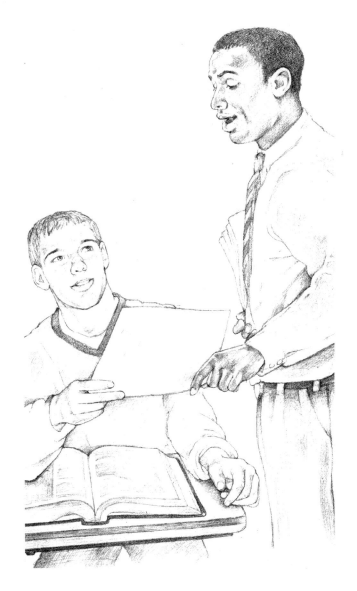

Griff knew what Coach Mann was going to say. He was going to tell Griff not to run on the track.

Griff slowly walked over to Coach Mann.

Coach Mann said, "Griff, I saw you at the track yesterday. I called to you. But you didn't hear me."

Griff didn't say anything.

Coach Mann said, "I wanted to talk to you. I hope you will try out for track this year."

That surprised Griff very much. He must have heard Coach Mann wrong.

"You want me to try out for track?" he asked.

"Yes, Griff. You are a good runner. But study hard to get good grades," Coach Mann said.

"OK. Maybe," Griff said.

He couldn't believe it. Coach Mann

wanted him to try out for track. Coach Mann must like him after all.

Griff felt good. But then he went to his history class.

Mrs. Dodd talked about the papers they had to write.

She said, "This class will meet in the media center tomorrow."

That was just great. Griff would have to go to the media center. He never went there.

Mrs. Dodd said, "You will work on your papers. Please use some of the books there. I want you to work while you are there. Do not waste time."

Griff had felt good after Coach Mann talked to him. But now he had to worry about his paper.

Chapter 8

It was the next day. Griff was in the media center. His history class was held there.

Mrs. Dodd said, "Work hard. Stay busy. And start now."

Griff put his books on a table. Then he went to a shelf and got a book. He took the book to the table. Griff sat down by himself.

Griff saw Laine. She looked at him. But he acted as if he didn't see her.

Laine went to a shelf. She got a book. Then she walked over to where he was.

Just great. Laine was going to sit at the table next to him. She would frown at him while he tried to work.

But she walked over to Griff's table.

Laine looked at Griff. She asked, "OK for me to sit here?"

"Yeah. I guess," Griff said.

He was too surprised to say anything else.

"You guess? You don't know?" Laine asked.

"Yeah. Sure. Sit down," Griff said.

"I'm not so sure I want to sit here now," Laine said.

Just great. He had made Laine mad.

"Do what you want to do," Griff said.

He knew she would anyway. But he didn't want Laine to think he cared what she did.

"I guess I will sit here," she said.

She sat down across from Griff.

Griff couldn't believe she sat there.

Laine said, "I think history is hard. What do you think?"

"Yeah," Griff said.

But he thought everything was hard.

Laine said, "We have a test in Mrs. Dodd's class tomorrow."

"Yeah. I know," Griff said.

How could he forget? But he sure would like to forget it.

Laine said, "I wish I had someone to study with. Last year I studied with Tess."

Tess was Laine's best friend.

"Yeah. I know," Griff said.

Why did Laine tell him that? He was in her class last year. So she knew he already knew about Tess.

He had wanted to study with them.

"Tess and I don't have the same teacher this year," Laine said.

Griff knew that too.

Laine and Griff didn't say anything for a few minutes.

Griff tilted his chair back against the wall. He acted as if he was reading a book. He looked at Laine a few times. She seemed to be reading a book. But he wasn't sure she was.

Then Laine asked, "Do you study history with anyone?"

"No," Griff said.

Why did she ask him that?

"Do you ever want to?" Laine asked.

"Yeah," Griff said.

He wanted to study with Ed. But Ed didn't have Mrs. Dodd for history.

Laine didn't say anything for a few minutes.

Then she asked, "Do you want to study with me sometime?"

That surprised Griff very much. He almost fell off his chair.

But he must have heard Laine wrong.

"What?" he asked.

At first Laine didn't answer. Griff wasn't sure she was going to answer.

Then she asked, "Do you want to study with me sometime?"

"Yeah. I guess," Griff said.

"You guess? You don't know?" Laine asked.

"Yeah. Sure. When?" Griff asked.

Griff couldn't believe he had asked her when.

Laine looked surprised too. She asked, "How about tonight?"

That surprised Griff even more. He almost fell off his chair again.

"OK," Griff said.

Griff couldn't believe it.

Laine had asked him for a date. Or at least he thought she had. It was only to study. But she had asked him over to her house. He never had a girl do that before. He always had to ask the girl for a date.

The last few days had been good for Griff. He couldn't believe it.

He had studied with Ed for his science test. And Ed said he could study with him again.

Griff had passed the science test. So Mr. Reese wasn't so bad after all.

Coach Mann wanted him to try out for track.

And now Laine had asked him for a date.

Griff was glad he didn't drop out of school.

He had thought this would be his worst year ever. But his senior year might not be so bad after all.